Unbroken

Treble Heart Books
1284 Overlook Dr.
Sierra Vista, AZ 85635-5512
http://www.trebleheartbooks.com

ISBN:1-931742-79-0

Thank you for choosing a sweet
romance novella
from
Treble Heart Books

Unbroken

Andrea Wilder

Treble Heart Books

Dedication

For Mom and Dad

Chapter One

"Excuse me. Is this chair taken?"

Paige shook her head and absently motioned to the vacant lounge beside her. "Help yourself."

She'd expected whoever it was to move the chair to wherever he'd come from. To her surprise, she heard him stretch out with a groan. Her curiosity piqued, she glanced out the side of her sunglasses to see who went with the weathered baritone voice.

Long, tanned legs led to a broad chest and even broader shoulders. Sun-streaked blond hair fell back from a strong jaw and a nose that had probably been broken more than once. In navy swim trunks and a pair of mega-bucks Ray-Bans, he looked like a surfer taking a snooze. He also looked very familiar.

With a mental shrug, Paige stuck a finger in her book to mark her place before reaching for her iced tea. Just before she opened her book again, the picture on the back caught her eye. She angled her gaze at the guy sprawled beside her.

The man in the chair was the man in the picture on the dust cover. No, he wasn't. He couldn't be. Nick Stafford was on a national signing tour. What would he be doing in Jamaica?

"So, how do you like it?"

The rugged voice broke into her mental tug-of-war, and Paige turned to face him. "I'm sorry?"

He propped himself on his elbow and pointed to her book. "How do you like it?"

"It's awesome! I love mysteries, and Derek Foster's the best P.I. character I've ever read." She paused and gathered her fleeting courage. "Since you asked, I was wondering—"

He held up his hand, and she fell silent.

"Yeah, I'm him. I'd appreciate it if you'd keep it to yourself, though. I just finished that tour, and I'm beat. I'm trying to relax for a few days before I head home."

"Oh, I won't tell anybody." She offered him her hand. "I'm Paige Ramsey. It's really cool to meet you."

She couldn't imagine why on earth he was chuckling.

"We've already met. In Charleston at one of my signings. You didn't give me your last name, though. Just Paige, for the autograph."

"Are you trying to tell me with all the people you meet, you actually remember me?"

He lay back down with a grin. He had the cutest dimple in his left cheek. "Yup."

She wasn't falling for that. A notorious ladies' man, he probably had a smooth line for every occasion. Of course, she'd expect something a little more cloquent than "yup."

"Okay, hotshot. What was I wearing?"

"Nice jeans, a pink polo shirt, and new Reeboks. And you smelled like flowers."

"Gardenias," Paige added, flattered beyond belief. "You *do* remember me."

"Wanna know why?"

"Sure." Her heart was racing, and she hoped she sounded casual. Nick Stafford *remembered* her.

"You were the only woman in that line who didn't paw at me or gush about how you *just loved* me." He aped a soprano Carolina accent and sighed.

"But they all bought a book, didn't they?"

"Yeah, they did. You actually read 'em, too. I was impressed with your critique of *Borrowed Time*."

"Thank you."

"You have a real pretty smile." He added an open, friendly one of his own.

"Thank you again."

She couldn't think of anything else to say, so she let her eyes drop back to her book. His book. She felt the heat on her cheeks as she blushed like a teenager with a crush.

Nick was quiet for so long, she thought he'd fallen asleep. Then he said, "It's such a beautiful day. Why aren't you out in the sun?"

"You don't want to see me when I've been in the sun. It's not pretty."

"A real English rose, huh?"

"Got that right."

"I like your accent," he told her.

"I don't have an accent. I like yours, though."

Laughing, he adjusted the back of his lounge chair and sat up. As he perused the crowded pool area, he frowned. Paige searched for what might have caused the change in his mood.

Four women were charging toward them, bouncing and swaying in bikinis that were at least a size too small. They were clearly aiming for Nick, and Paige felt a twinge of pity. He was thirty-five and one of the hottest authors around. He'd also been divorced twice and linked with half the actresses in Hollywood.

What you'd call a catch. These four appeared intent on reeling him in like a ten-pound rainbow trout.

"I knew it was him," the leggy blonde declared in a Southern honey drawl, plopping down on his chair. She had the audacity to put her hand on his thigh. "Could we get a picture of the five of us? Nobody will believe we met you unless we have proof."

"Sure." Nick gave her an easy smile. "You have a photographer in mind?"

She turned to Paige and held out her camera. "Sugar, would you be an absolute *angel* and take our picture? Maybe five or six, just to make sure they come out."

Paige glanced at Nick, and he nodded. "It's all right, Paige. Go ahead."

She took the camera and stood a few paces back while the women arranged themselves around Nick. He looked like a sheikh surrounded by his harem. The women fussed over him a while longer, then fluttered away with promises to send him copies of the pictures.

"Y'know, I came over here 'cause it was less crowded," Nick grumbled, staring out at the horizon. He seemed to recover a little, because he smiled. "I love the ocean. It's so huge, even those monstrous cruise ships get swallowed up. The waves keep rolling, life keeps going." After a few quiet moments, he turned to her. "What do you do?"

"I'm the assistant manager of a bookstore in Charleston." When he laughed, she tried not to take it personally. "What?"

"Your name's Paige, and you work in a bookstore. You don't think that's funny?"

"I guess."

Actually, she thought it was pathetic. She had a plain old name and a plain old job. He was like a seagull soaring above the waves. She was like a sandpiper stuck on the beach. She'd decided to do something about that, though, if only for the next few days.

"Do you have any idea how long it's been since I laughed like that?"

"Is this a trick question?"

"Too long. I think you're about the sweetest, most down-to-earth woman I've ever met." He paused, gazing thoughtfully at her. "No, I take that back. You *are* the sweetest, most down-to-earth woman I've ever met. Are you free for lunch?"

Paige swallowed to make sure her answer wouldn't come in a stuttering squeak. "Yes, I am."

"Would you like to join me?"

She couldn't keep back an elated smile. "Very much."

"Great. Do you mind if I get in a few laps before we go?"

Now she was confused. There was a huge buffet just a few yards away. "Go where?"

"To my room. I can't eat while I'm signing autographs." His bright expression dimmed. "Unless you'd rather eat down here."

"No, your room's fine. Whatever's best for you."

He must have heard the nervous skip in her voice. Shaking his head, he gave her a wry grin. "You know, I just realized how that sounded. I've got a suite with a nice view of the ocean from the verandah. I thought we could eat out there."

"Sure. I knew that." Because no way in a million years would Nick Stafford even *think* of inviting her up to his room for anything else. One of the drawbacks of looking like everybody's favorite little sister.

He slipped off his sunglasses and set them on the table between their chairs. Paige had thought she'd imagined the warm color of his eyes when she met him before. Now she noticed they perfectly matched the crystal blue water just offshore. Knowing how much he loved the ocean, it seemed right somehow.

"Thanks for being such a sport." He winked at her. "I promise to behave myself."

As he strutted off, Paige admired the back of him, which was just as tan and well-muscled as the front. He dove into a nearby pool, surfacing a few yards out and tossing his hair back with a spray of water. With powerful strokes, he swam the length of the pool and turned like an Olympic freestyler.

He'd behave. Paige balanced her elbow on the armrest and dropped her chin into her hand with a sigh. Most of the men she dated said something like that. Then, at the end of the evening, they pecked her on the cheek and drove off, never to be seen again.

Just once, she'd like to go out with a guy who didn't behave.

As they strolled down the hall, Nick garnered plenty of feminine attention, which Paige could easily understand. The sight of him in wet swim trunks would stop the heart of any woman over ten and still breathing. He unlocked his door and put a hand on her waist to guide her into his suite. He was warm and damp and entirely too close for comfort.

Nick reached into a dresser drawer and pulled out some dry clothes. Then he picked up the room service menu and handed it to her.

"I'll go change, and then we can order lunch. Just decide what you want."

What I want isn't on the menu. But the bathroom door closed before she could summon the courage to tell him so. Of course, he could have stood there for a month, and she never would have told him that.

While she read through the list of light meals, she fought to calm her racing heart. She was being ridiculous. Nick was a handsome, charming man who'd invited her to have lunch with him. Of course, her reaction might have something to do with the fact that handsome, charming men didn't usually look at her twice, much less ask her to lunch.

Paige gave herself a mental shake. He probably appreciated her not asking for his autograph, and this was his way of thanking her. She tried not to look through the open door at the rumpled bed, tried not to think of him sleeping there.

What did a man like him dream about? The next book? The next woman he'd indulge himself with? In magazines and on the entertainment shows, she saw the women he dated and, presumably, slept with. They were glittering Hollywood. She was Charleston beach house. No comparison.

"Find something you like?"

His question jolted her out of her reverie, and she tried to sound casual. "The seafood salad looks good. How about you?"

"That was my choice, too." He motioned her to the balcony. "I'll be there in a minute."

She went through the cozy sitting room, out the sliding doors to the veranda. He was on the phone, and she heard him add iced tea to their order. He must have seen her drinking it earlier. Was there anything more attractive than a man who picked up on what you liked and remembered?

He joined her at the railing. "Ten minutes, they said."

"That's fine. I'm enjoying the view."

"Yeah, me, too." He tipped his head and smiled at her. Not a *come on, baby let's hit the sheets* kind of grin, but another warm smile. To Paige's very pleasant surprise, Nick was a really nice guy. A bit jaded, maybe, but he was polite to those women earlier and to all the people who'd stopped them in the hallway.

"I noticed you're not carrying a pen. Is that so you don't have to sign so many autographs?"

"Yeah. I don't usually mind all that, but sometimes I just

need a break. I'm glad people like my work, though. That's why I do it."

"I thought it was all those big-time publishing contracts."

His cheek dimpled into a sheepish grin. "Well, they're nice, but I don't need that much money. Mostly, I just love to write. For a long time, I did it for nothing."

"They profiled you last month in *Books*. I saw you on the cover with your house and car. You'd need a lot of money for those."

"Well, the Beemer's mine, but not the house. It's my parents'."

"Wow. What do they do?"

"They're retired now, but they still teach a little at the college where they used to work. When I sold *Time of Mind*, I bought the house for them. It's in La Mirada. Ever since I was a kid, my mom wanted that place. There's a six-car garage and a shop out back, where my dad restores vintage cars with a couple of his buddies."

So he was generous, too. She liked him more all the time. "And you live in Malibu."

"Yeah. I love it there. I live way up the beach where it's quieter." Nick looked out at the water, as if he were imagining his own view. "I write out on the deck in the mornings, listening to the ocean and the birds. It's one of the most beautiful, peaceful places I've ever seen."

"It sounds kind of lonely, though."

"No, I like having a place I can go and hang out. Walk around naked if I want to," he added with a wicked grin.

Narrowing her eyes, she did her best to glare at him. "You just had to say that, didn't you?"

Laughter trailed behind him as he went to let the waiter in. When the man set their lunch on the table, Paige's jaw dropped at the ten-dollar tip Nick gave him. After the waiter left, Nick explained, "I waited tables for a couple of years during college. They don't get paid much for all the crap they take."

He stood behind one of the white wicker chairs until she sat down. Then he pushed her chair in and sat in the other one.

"Are you sure you're from California?" she asked as she unfolded the damask flower that became her napkin.

"Yeah. Why?"

"Well, with your manners, you could be a proper Southern gentleman." She drawled heavily over the last few words, batting her eyelashes for effect.

"My mom'll be glad to hear it. How's your salad?"

"Delicious. And thank you for the iced tea. It was real nice of you to remember."

He took a sip of his and set the glass down. "What I remembered was how good yours looked earlier. I'd just spent ten minutes debating plot points with a couple from Denver, and I was parched."

They ate in silence for a while. Then Paige's curiosity got the better of her. "Could I ask you a question?"

"Shoot."

"Are you working on a new book?"

He grinned, nodding while he swallowed a mouthful of salad. "I'm always working on a new book."

"What's it called?"

He stared somberly at her. "Keep a secret?"

"Mmm-hmm."

"I have no idea. My agent, Anita, names 'em. I call 'em one, two, three, four, five, six." She laughed, and he leaned his elbows on the table, looking very earnest. "No, really. I'm awful with titles."

"I like the time thing, though. *Time of Mind*, *Broken Time*, *Stitch in Time*. But my favorite is the one I haven't read yet."

He chewed, studying her intently. "You're serious."

"Of course, I am. In every book, Derek gets more interesting. We find out more about his past and what's in his future. Probably because the same is happening with you."

"Guess you're right. I never thought about it."

"You're much better now than you were a few years ago." His eyebrow shot up, and she quickly added, "At writing."

As a pretty blush crept up her cheeks, Nick couldn't believe it. When was the last time he'd seen a woman honestly blush? Her dark hair hung down her back in a thick French braid, little curls around her temples framing eyes the color of cornflowers. He couldn't remember ever meeting a woman so natural and easy to talk to.

"So, Paige." He leaned back in his chair and crossed his bare feet on the railing. "You seem to know all about me. Tell me about you."

"You wouldn't be interested in that. It's way too boring."

"Try me."

She slipped off her sandals and sat cross-legged in her chair. "Well, I was born and raised in Charleston. I went to UNC for English Lit."

"Go, Tarheels," he commented, rewarded with an approving smile. "Do you have any brothers or sisters?"

"Four brothers, all older. I'm the only girl."

"Daddy's angel, right?"

"Pretty much."

Nick groaned. "Don't tell me. He's big as a bear with a temper to match."

"Yeah. And Mom's about the size of a leprechaun. She stands on a chair when they argue."

"You have a knack for painting pictures. You should try writing sometime." He knew what that shy smile meant. "Have you?"

"I've written some fairy tales, mostly for my niece Hannah. She does the drawings, and I write stories to go with them."

"That's cool. How many have you done?"

"Not as many as I'd like. I write them out longhand and type them on the computer at work. I have a lot more ideas than time."

He chuckled. "That sounds familiar."

They chatted pleasantly through lunch and long after, like two old friends who'd just run into each other after a few years apart. Her light-hearted company was so refreshing, he hated to let her leave.

But she stood and retrieved her sandals from under the table. "I really should go so you can get ready for dinner. You must have plans for tonight."

Reluctantly, he walked her to the door. "Actually, I thought I'd eat here. After what happened earlier, I'd rather not run into my worst critic or my biggest fan."

Paige glanced around, then hesitantly at him. "Nick, I know it's not my place to say this, but spending all your time in your room is no way to enjoy Jamaica."

"It's a really nice room, though." He was trying to look on the bright side but, from her sympathetic smile, he knew he'd only managed to sound pathetic.

"No place is nice enough if you're trapped there."

Nick couldn't think of anything to say. She'd nailed him but good.

For the first few years, he'd enjoyed the perks that came with his success. It was fun and, as an only child, he loved the attention. When his second divorce put him back on the market, the focus on his personal life intensified, and being a celebrity started wearing him out. A few hours ago, he'd been looking forward to a quiet evening alone. Now that was the last thing he wanted.

"Paige, you're right. Thanks for clearing my head for me." He did a mock bow. "In return, may I accompany you to dinner?"

"Please," she muttered, shoving him out of her way. "Give me half an hour. Room 640."

Nick's jaw dropped, and he pointed at the locked door in the side wall. "You're in there?" When she nodded, he asked, "When did you check in?"

"Yesterday."

"You were in there all last night, and I never knew it?"

"I'm very quiet," she informed him. "Did you know you talk to yourself a lot?"

"Writer's occupational hazard. Sorry if I bothered you."

"You didn't. I just figured you had somebody in here."

"Right. Like who?"

She shrugged, her eyes going to the plush emerald carpet. "Whoever you wanted."

Her response was so quiet, Nick wasn't sure she wanted him to hear it. He didn't care what most people thought of him. They were wrong most of the time, and he'd gotten used to it. It came with the territory. But for some crazy reason, he wanted Paige Ramsey to know what kind of man he truly was.

"Paige." When she looked up, he smiled reassurance. "Do you really think I'm like that?"

She gazed at him for a long moment. Then she wrapped him in a warm smile and stood on tiptoe to kiss his cheek. "Not anymore."

She breezed past him into the hall. In her wake, she left the delicate scent of gardenias.

Chapter Two

She was about to have dinner with a real, honest-to-goodness author. Not just any author but the one who was number six on *People* magazine's most beautiful people list. Last year, he was number eight.

"You, however, wouldn't even make the top thousand," Paige grumbled at her reflection. She was wearing the dress she only wore at Christmas, so it still looked new even though it was several years old. It was burgundy crepe, with a sleeveless velvet bodice and a short jacket that closed with a silver star. It was very pretty, and it suited her coloring well. Still, she couldn't help wishing she had a strappy little black number, with knock-him-dead black and silver stiletto heels.

Oh, well. She'd make do.

Should she wear the jacket? Paige slipped it off and assessed her reflection again. With so much skin exposed, she felt half naked. She'd never wear it this way at home, but then, all those people knew how reserved she was. The Paige they knew would die of embarrassment dressed like this.

She was still debating when she heard a quiet knock on the side door. Tossing the jacket onto a chair, she called up her courage and boldly turned the knob.

Nick looked incredible. His single-breasted suit was midnight blue, and the contrast with the white shirt enhanced his tan and the color of his eyes. Those eyes swept over her with a practiced glance, twinkling with what she hoped was approval and not amusement.

"You look great." He held his arm out for her. "Ready?"

Actually, she would have liked to do some more primping, but she didn't want to keep him waiting. She nodded and took his arm, keenly aware she was probably the least glamorous woman he'd ever dated. At least she'd had the sense to ditch the jacket.

While they waited for the elevator, he turned to her with a broad grin. "Hey, nobody stopped me. You must be my good luck charm."

"More likely, they were so busy trying to figure out why on earth you're with me, they didn't have time to dig out a pen."

Crossing his arms, he scowled at her. "What's that supposed to mean?"

"Nick, I'm hardly in a league with Amity Farrell or Chelsea Remington," she told him, mentioning two actresses he'd been photographed with recently.

"Count your blessings, sweetheart," he muttered as they walked onto the elevator.

She had no idea what he meant, but she liked his disgruntled tone.

"What are you grinning at?" he asked with a grin of his own.

"Nothing." She didn't stop smiling, though. "It doesn't sound like you think much of them, is all."

"They weren't what I expected. Let's leave it at that."

Paige was ridiculously pleased to hear that, but in a prim tone, she told him, "It's really none of my business."

As the elevator doors slid open, he replied, "No, but I've been telling you all kinds of secrets today. What's one more?"

On their way to the dining room, they passed the gleaming windows of the hotel's jewelry boutique. *Oceania* arched over the door in gold script letters. Paige tried to keep walking but ended up in front of the glittering display. She managed to resist the urge to press her nose to the glass, but it was a near thing. Each unique piece was beautifully handcrafted, with a card signed by the artist.

Her gaze was drawn to a bracelet of leaping gold dolphins. Exquisitely tooled, it probably exceeded her souvenir budget by several digits. Paige thought about the credit card in her black evening bag, sorely tempted to buy the bracelet simply because she wanted it.

Then she thought about the new clutch her car needed and the things she'd bought for her vacation. But that bracelet was so pretty.

"See something you like?"

Nick seemed perfectly comfortable pressed against her back, his chin resting on top of her head as he peered in the window. She hoped he didn't notice the excited hammering of her heart.

"They're all very nice," she answered, starting to walk down the hallway.

He caught her hand and pulled her back. "Which one, Paige?"

"None in particular. They're all beautiful."

He smoothed her hair back over her shoulders, his fingers gently brushing her skin. But the emotion twinkling in his eyes wasn't desire. It was fondness.

Before she could figure out if she was pleased or disappointed, he teased, "Y'know, I've been around the block a few times, and I've seen that look. Which one?"

She decided there was no harm in pointing it out to him.

"Very pretty. And there's a necklace that goes with it."

"And earrings," she added, embarrassed when she realized she'd spoken out loud.

"And earrings." He chuckled as his finger followed the curve of her jaw. "You're blushing. Why?"

Paige didn't answer at first, but not because she couldn't. She didn't want him to stop caressing her cheek. When he drew his hand away, she bit back a sigh. "I didn't mean to hint."

"I know. Would you like them, Paige?"

"Of course not." Gathering the few remaining shreds of her dignity, she resolutely turned away from him and the window full of temptation. "We should go in for dinner."

"Okay."

He rested his arm lightly around her shoulders as they strode through the archway into the restaurant. Paige had to remind herself not to stop and gawk. She felt completely out of place in such an elegant setting. Nick was accustomed to sophisticated women dressed in silk and diamonds, not klutzes who tripped over their high heels.

The center atrium was several stories tall, its beveled dome framing a dusky sky. A sweeping staircase joined the two posh levels, the curving brass banister polished to mirror perfection. Chandeliers hung over round tables set for six, and cozy tables for two lined the walls. On the damask tablecloths, gleaming silverware flanked fine china and crystal. The view through the expanse of windows was a fabulous Caribbean sunset. An artist couldn't have painted a more breathtaking scene.

On their way through the dining room, she noticed each table held a bouquet of pink camellias. But at their table, white gardenias overflowed a crystal vase etched with stars. It was the only one.

"You did this," she gasped, delighted by his thoughtfulness.

"Yeah." He pulled the tufted chair out for her. "I'm glad you like them."

Paige sat and smiled over her shoulder at him as he pushed in her chair. She'd never been treated like a queen before. "They're beautiful, Nick. Thank you."

He sat across from her. "I figured it was the least I could do after taking up your whole afternoon like that."

"There's nothing I would've rather done. I enjoyed getting to know you. I never thought I'd see you again, much less get to talk to you for so long."

"I enjoyed it, too. Very much." He turned his attention to the wine list. "What would you like?"

"I'm not really a wine person."

He laughed. "When you said that, you wrinkled your nose like a little kid turning down broccoli."

"Sorry."

"Don't be. It's cute."

He thought she was cute. Wonderful.

"I was curious about something," he went on in a conversational tone.

"What's that?"

"You don't really seem like the Caribbean type. How is it you're in Jamaica?"

"My parents gave me the trip for my th—for my birthday."

From his crooked grin, he'd filled in the word she cut short. At least he was nice enough not to mention it. "When was your birthday?"

"February fourteenth."

"A Valentine's baby." With a smile, he lifted his water goblet. "Happy birthday, Paige."

"Thank you."

Nick tapped his glass against hers, a pensive look coming into his eyes as they settled on hers. "Do you have any idea—"

His voice trailed off, and Paige held her breath, waiting for him to finish. But a movement took their attention from each other. A waiter stood beside the table, ready to take their order. If he found their behavior odd, he showed no sign of it. He probably saw lots of couples gazing across the table, lost in each other.

Paige wished she were used to it. Then maybe her heart would quit tripping over itself every time Nick looked at her.

"Do you like lobster?"

"Oh, I *love* lobster." Then she tried to compose herself to sound a little more grown-up. "That sounds great."

Nick closed his menu, handing it and hers to the waiter. "You heard the lady. And a pitcher of iced tea, please."

"Yes, sir." With that, the waiter moved on.

Smiling, Nick stood and offered her his arm. "Would you like to dance?"

Paige looked across the parquet floor at the dancing couples. They were so graceful, moving easily together while they talked. "I'm not a very good dancer."

"Neither am I." He gave her a devilish grin. "Don't tell anybody."

"Another deep, dark secret?"

As they strolled onto the dance floor, he said, "Keep it up, I won't have any left."

For some crazy reason, she liked the sound of that. After a few clumsy steps, he suggested she let him lead.

"I was leading?"

His ringing laugh bounced around the dining room, and she caught several shocked looks aimed in their direction. She felt the color rising on her cheeks, and she buried her face in his chest.

His arm stayed around her waist, but his other hand slid under her chin, tipping her face up. "I'm sorry. Did I embarrass you?"

"I'm not used to so much attention," she stammered, her eyes widening under his warm scrutiny. Was he actually going to kiss her? She had no doubt she was growing redder by the second.

"I can't imagine that, pretty as you are."

He ticked her nose with his finger, and Paige swallowed a disappointed sigh as he took her hand again. Nick was being a perfect gentleman. She should be grateful he wasn't the ravenous womanizer the tabloids made him out to be.

"What do you have planned for the rest of your vacation, Paige?"

"I thought I'd finish your new book."

He laughed again. "Besides that."

She assessed him carefully, then decided to go for broke and really answer his question. "I want to completely get away from my life."

He gave her a slow nod of understanding. "Yeah. Me, too."

Paige smiled and rested her cheek on the soft lapel of his jacket. She breathed in the scent of the ocean tinged with cologne. On him, the combination seemed just right.

Her cheek vibrated as his deep voice broke into her thoughts. "So, how do you go about getting away from your life?"

"I'd like to do things I don't usually do."

"Like what?"

"I don't know. Reach for the stars, do something exciting."

He dropped her into a dip, and she shrieked, grabbing his shoulders to keep from falling. Then he drew her upright and close against him. Much closer than she'd been before.

"Exciting enough?"

She could only nod. Hopefully, he'd think her deep flush was from the dancing.

"Are you going into town tomorrow?" he asked.

"Definitely. I can't wait to see Dunn's River Falls. The tour group leaves at nine."

"I could show you around, unless you'd rather go with the group."

He hadn't planned on sightseeing during this trip. Been there, done that. Many times. But something told him seeing Ocho Rios with Paige would be like watching a little girl on Christmas morning. Something else told him he was taking up too much of her time. She was on vacation, too. She hadn't bargained on keeping him company.

"Oh, I'd much rather go with you. I was reading the brochure, and there's a place where you can swim with dolphins. I've gone on whale watches, and sometimes we saw dolphins, too. They're so playful, I think it would be awesome to get right in and swim with them."

"I'll see if I can dig us up a couple of spots at Dolphin Cove." That was probably next to impossible this time of year, but it was amazing how fame bypassed the system. He didn't usually take advantage of his notoriety but for one of Paige's incredible smiles, he couldn't think of anything he wouldn't do.

"They have a great outdoor bazaar, too," he told her.

"I'm not much of a shopper."

He'd never heard a woman say that, and it took him a few seconds to recover from the shock. "That's fine. We could go snorkeling instead. Do you know how?"

Paige rolled her eyes. "We snorkel in the Atlantic Ocean, too, you know. The icebergs don't generally roll in until January."

She tacked on a sassy face, which made him laugh. The surprise of hearing his own laughter was finally beginning to wear off. "Thank you, Paige."

"For what?"

"For today. For reminding me women like you still exist."

"Nick, who in the world have you been hanging out with?" When he shrugged, she cocked her head and gave him an impish smile. "Maybe you need to spend a little more time with me."

Returning that smile was the easiest thing he'd done in a long, long time.

"It's not hard, Paige." Nick settled her on a tall chrome stool in front of the blackjack table. "The dealer puts a card face down for each player, then one face up for the house. Then she puts a card face up for each of you, then another for the house. You're the only one who knows what your first card is."

"And I'm supposed to get to twenty-one," she added as the dealer converted Nick's casino card into chips.

"Right. Or as close as you can without going over. That's a bust."

"Yes, it is."

Nick's gaze had dropped from her eyes to the sweetheart neckline of her dress. Yanking his attention back to her face, he saw her lips tilt into a knowing feminine smirk. She hadn't gone to freshen up once, so he knew that very appealing pink was their natural color.

She had a gently curved mouth, made for long, maddening kisses. A woman who knew how to use a mouth like that could drive a man crazy before he knew what was happening to him. Of course, she'd been doing that all evening.

But that wasn't what he was here for. Paige wasn't the kind of woman you tumbled into bed with and left behind. And, for the sake of his sanity, he'd sworn off the heavy stuff a long time ago.

He climbed onto the stool beside her and focused on the chips stacked in front of them.

"Okay, now for the betting." He tapped the purple chips. "These are five hundred."

"Dollars?"

"The blacks are a hundred," he continued. "Greens are twenty-five, reds are five, and whites are a dollar. So, go ahead."

"Can I watch first?" Paige glanced at the dealer, who smiled encouragement.

"Sure can, honey," the woman assured her in a melodic Jamaican accent. "When you want to join in, you just let me know." Then she turned to Nick. "Sir?"

In answer, he carelessly tossed two purple chips into his betting circle. When the hand was dealt, Nick had the queen of diamonds showing. Then he tipped up his cards. His table card was the ace of hearts. He waited for the others to play out their hands, then flipped over his ace. "Blackjack."

He played several more hands, winning two more with twenty-one. He'd never had luck like this. Of all the games in the casino, the players' odds were best in blackjack, but this was incredible.

Then he noticed the player to Paige's left was eyeing her with great interest.

"Are you his good luck charm, angel face?" The guy swiveled to face her, smiling a little more warmly than Nick could tolerate.

"Yeah, she is." Nick leveled a glare at him. It took everything he had not to drop a protective arm around her bare shoulders.

The man pulled away, holding up his hands. "Just looking for some luck, that's all."

"Look somewhere else."

The idiot laughed, glancing around the table, then back at him. "You're serious."

Nick stood, placing himself between the jerk and Paige, his hand on her shoulder. It was a casual move no man in his right mind could misinterpret. Without another word, the stranger scooped up his chips and fled to the relative safety of the craps table.

When he sat back down, Nick was astonished to find Paige glowering at him. "When you haul the sabertooth tiger back to the cave, would you like it broiled or baked?"

"He was being rude," he said with a dismissive shrug.

"So were you."

"But I was rude to a guy who's half-drunk already and won't remember it in the morning. He was rude to a lady."

"Why don't you just take him outside and beat him up?"

"That's a little extreme, don't you think?" He settled his arm across the back of her stool and leaned closer to her. "But if that's what you want, I'll think about it."

"You'd beat somebody up just because I wanted you to?"

"How do you think I got this?" He tapped the crooked bone in his nose.

"You sound like my brothers."

He grinned as he sat back down. "Why am I getting the impression that's not a compliment?"

"It's not. Fighting is stupid. Fighting over a girl is infantile."

"Oo, good word." He chuckled as he motioned to a cruising waitress. "Mind if I use it sometime?"

"Of course not. I didn't make it up."

"Would you like something?" he asked when the waitress stopped beside them.

"No."

He gave the waitress his order, returning her lip-licking smile with a charming one of his own. His insolence was beginning to irritate Paige. Where did all this macho attitude come from, anyway? Alone with her, he'd seemed so laid-back, as interested in her as she was in him. When the server strolled off, and as he loosened his paisley tie, Paige heard him sigh.

"Thanks for a nice evening, Nick," she said as she got down from her stool.

"Where are you going?"

His puzzled tone stopped her in mid-stride. How could he not know? Maybe his other dates didn't mind being treated like number seventy-two in line at the deli, but she didn't like it one bit.

"Obviously, I'm cramping your style."

"My style?" he echoed, shaking his head. "What are you talking about?"

"Barbie." Paige motioned in the general direction of the bar. "If I go, you can hang out with her."

"What? You don't like blondes?"

"Natural ones are fine."

"That's kind of narrow-minded, don't you think?"

"I think you're broad-minded enough for both of us." When he grinned, she snarled, "What's so funny?"

"Broad-minded. Broads, women, I get it."

"Oh, that's perfect. I'm trying to make a point, and you think I'm joking."

Just then, the waitress returned with his drink. On the bar napkin, she'd scribbled "Heather" with a phone number after it. Nick sent her off with a nice tip and a grin.

Totally disgusted, Paige turned on her heel and left.

Paige stood on her balcony, staring at the moonlit ocean. A few boats were anchored offshore, their cabin lights winking while laughter floated in on the warm breeze. It ruffled through the skirt of her nightgown, helping to settle her nerves.

She'd made a complete fool of herself. Nick Stafford was exactly the way he'd been portrayed by the media. Her big mistake had been thinking otherwise. She just couldn't understand why when they were alone, he seemed so nice and in a crowd, he seemed …

The way everybody expected him to be.

"Don't go there, Paige," she muttered, shaking her head. "People can't always be what you want."

She heard a soft knock on her side door and looked over her shoulder. It was after midnight, and she was tempted to ignore it. Then her curiosity got the better of her good sense, and she went to open the door.

Nick stood there, his designer jacket slung over his shoulder like a flannel shirt. While she waited for him to say something, she couldn't help admiring the picture he made leaning against the doorjamb.

"I was thinking about what you said," he began in an apologetic voice.

Hardly daring to believe she'd heard him right, Paige forgot she was in her pajamas and stared up at him. "You were?"

"Yeah, I was. I didn't mean to insult you, but I could see how you might've taken things wrong."

"Any woman would have. They just might not have said anything."

"That's one of the things I like about you. I never have to wonder what you're thinking."

His approving tone made her laugh. "Most men consider that a character flaw."

"Not me." He cocked his head with a wry grin. "Does this mean I'm forgiven?"

"For not doing anything? Sure."

Now what? Should she ask him in? What would he think if she did? The answer to that was pathetically obvious. He'd think she was a tramp, but she really didn't want him to go. He intrigued and baffled her at the same time. All night long, he'd reached for her, then pulled away. She couldn't shake the feeling that this handsome, lonely man needed something he couldn't buy.

He needed her.

Her mind and heart in agreement, Paige opened her door wide and stood with her back against it. Heart racing wildly, she tried to look calm, like she did this all the time. "Would you like to come in?"

"You usually ask guys in on the first date?" he asked with a disapproving scowl.

"No, just you."

He didn't respond to that, and she studied him in silence. She saw pain in his eyes, etched into them like scars. When he ventured out from behind his cool personality, he made her think of a wounded little boy, looking for someone to give him a hug.

She reached her hand to his jaw, and it clenched under her touch. "Nick, who did this to you? Who hurt you so much you can't trust me?"

He removed her hand from his cheek and kissed her palm. His eyes had gone steely blue, the hurt firmly locked away. "Paige, I'm gonna give you the same speech I give everybody. I'm not looking for anything serious, but I can never have too many friends. Can we be friends?"

"I thought we were."

Nick almost kissed the puzzled frown from her lips. But he knew if he did, he'd never stop. Some deep instinct warned him this was a woman he could lose himself in, and that was the last thing he needed. He was still clawing his way back from the last time.

She turned and walked into her room, welcoming him in if he wanted to follow her, acknowledging his right to leave. He didn't know what to think.

When he finally followed her, he found her looking over the contents of her little refrigerator. "So, are you a cookies and milk kind of guy or a mini-bar kind of guy?"

"Both. Nothing like chocolate chip cookies dipped in Kahlua."

"I bet." She laughed. "Is that what you want?"

He wanted to peel her out of that pretty nightgown and make love to her. Hold her in his arms while she slept, waking once in a while to be sure she wasn't a dream. In his imagination, he saw her sleepy morning smile, and the vivid picture rattled him.

"Thanks, but I think I'll take a rain check. It's pretty late, and I should get going." He glanced at the open doors between their rooms. "Make sure you lock your door."

She stood and faced him, a teasing smile on her face. "What's the matter? Afraid I'll come in and ravage you while you're sleeping?"

"Something like that."

"Well, I promise I won't. You can trust me."

"But can *you* trust *me*?" He'd intended to match her light-hearted tone, but even to his own ears, he sounded way too serious.

"You told me you're not like that. I believe you."

He folded his arms, inexplicably angry. "You're not gonna lock that door, are you?"

"No, I'm not." She seemed totally unfazed by his fit of temper. "But you have a door, too, Nick. You can lock it if you want to."

Something told him there was more to that quiet comment than the words. Something in her eyes, something he couldn't begin to deduce at one o'clock in the morning.

With a resigned sigh, he leaned in to kiss her cheek. "Good night, Paige."

He walked into his sitting room and turned on the lights. He closed the door behind him and almost turned the deadbolt the way he always did when he traveled. Knowing there was a stranger on the other side of the wall made him uneasy.

He left the door unlocked, mostly so Paige wouldn't harass him about it in the morning.

The bedspread and frothy green sheets were already turned down for the night. Tossing his Armani jacket and tie onto a green club chair, he sat on the edge of the bed to slip off his shoes and socks. While he unbuttoned his shirt, he noticed the pillows he'd wrestled with during his nap were lined up again, companionably side by side at the head of the bed.

He only needed one of them.

And he needed a drink, he grumbled silently, hunkering down to assess the mini bar situation. Dropping some ice cubes into a crystal glass, he poured in two generous fingers of Scotch, then two more. Uncharacteristically restless, he wandered through the sliding doors toward the comforting sounds of the ocean. Arms balanced on the balcony railing, Nick sipped his drink while he contemplated the rippling reflection of the moon.

Sweet, thoughtful Paige Ramsey thoroughly surprised him. He'd gotten caught up in the simple pleasure of her. She was bright, interested in everything. He found himself smiling just thinking about her. It had been a long time since he took a woman at face value, instead of analyzing her for flaws and gauging how long it would be before she left him.

He had his ex-wives to thank for that. His first failed marriage had made him cautious. The second had paralyzed him. The decree was pinned above his cluttered storyboard, to remind him a long-term relationship just wasn't in the cards for him. His writing demanded too much of his time, and there wasn't enough of him left over for a commitment to anybody.

Nick wished he could have them both, but it would take an exceedingly understanding woman to be the wife of an author on the rise. His career would have to be as important to her as it was to him. That was a lot to ask. Apparently, too much.

A man in his position could have company whenever he wanted it. Beautiful, obliging women who gladly accepted what he offered them. An elegant dinner, a moonlit drive along the coast, a night tangling the sheets. It kept the male part of him more or less satisfied, but the man in him longed for more.

He wanted a woman like Paige. A woman who wasn't enchanted by the trappings of his success. Someone kind and understanding, who enjoyed his company just for the sake of having it. Someone who respected his career and how important it was to him. Sex he could find anywhere.

Love was what eluded him.

With a grimace, Nick emptied his glass and set it on the table. He was brooding. Well, at least he could make it productive. He settled into one of the chairs, crossing his bare feet on the other. He leaned his head back and stared out at the stars, his mind going to the outline for his latest project.

Closing his eyes, he tried to picture the next scene. Instead, Paige's face swam into view, her starry blue eyes sparkling as he heard her laughter. A gentle breeze brushed through his hair and, in his memory, he felt the softness of her cheek as he kissed her good night.

He sighed, trying to push the vivid image away. Then he changed tracks, mentally putting words with what he was feeling. As one idea flowed into another, Nick realized he was on the kind of roll no writer could ignore.

Anita had commandeered his laptop in Charleston, ordering him to totally relax for five days. But that didn't mean he couldn't write.

Hurrying back inside, Nick grabbed a pen and the pad of hotel stationery from the desk.

Maybe it was time for cool, detached Derek Foster to want something he couldn't have. See how *he* handled it.

Chapter Three

"Nick, are you in there?"

"Yeah, hang on."

He finished the sentence he was working on before opening their adjoining door. Dressed in faded cutoffs and a sleeveless yellow blouse, Paige looked fresh as a daisy and twice as pretty. That was good. He could use that line.

"Just a second." He scrawled the phrase on a scrap of paper, tucking it in the corner of the mirror with a collection of other unrelated ramblings.

Paige followed him inside and frowned as she surveyed his room. For the first time, he noticed it was a wreck. Several half-empty coffee cups were on the low table, surrounded by crumpled sheets of paper. The ham and cheese omelet he'd ordered at five-thirty sat untouched on the love seat, which was strewn with papers.

"What are you doing?" she asked.

"Sorry about the mess. I had this great idea last night, and I'm seeing where it goes. That reminds me. What's your middle name?"

"Ellen. Why?"

He shrugged and logged the name into his mental file. "Just curious."

"What's yours?"

"Charles."

She cocked her head at him and grinned. "Nicholas Charles? Like in *The Thin Man*?"

"Yeah. Mom loves those old movies. Nick and Nora downing martinis and solving crimes." Then he chuckled. "You're one of the few people under fifty who gets the deal about my name."

"Oh, *The Thin Man* is a classic. It was the first mystery novel I ever read, and I was hooked. Hammett had a way with that stuff. *The Maltese Falcon* was great, too."

"Sam Spade was my dad's favorite. Big Bogart fan."

She gave him a once-over, and Nick realized he was still in his trousers, his shirt untucked and hanging open. He ran a hand over his rough cheek and grimaced. "I must look like death warmed over."

"You haven't been to bed yet?"

He heard the horror in her tone, and he chuckled. "No, but I got inspired. See, there's this—" He stopped abruptly. She wasn't there to be bored with his stupendous plot twists. She wanted the tour of Ocho Rios he'd promised her.

To his amazement, Paige cleared a spot on one of the cushions and sat down, Indian style. She looked genuinely interested, her eyes dancing with the same excitement he felt rushing through him. No, that was probably caffeine.

"What?" she prompted.

"You don't want to hear this."

"I'd love to hear it. If you want to tell me."

"I don't know," he teased. "Can you keep a secret?"

She nodded eagerly, and he sprawled out on the floor, hands

under his head. "Well, Derek sees this woman in the crowd at Heathrow airport."

As he went on, Paige curled into the corner of the love seat, her cheek pillowed on her hand while she listened to his developing story. She asked several intelligent questions and even pointed out some logistical flaws.

"You know my books better than I do." He grinned up at her. "So, what do you think of this one?"

"It's great, but why the romance? Isn't Derek a confirmed ladies' man since his wife died?"

"It's time for him to get over it."

"I agree. Nobody should be alone that long. It's sad."

Her compassion rattled him, and he studied her intently. Melinda Foster's tragic death had coincided with the demise of his second marriage, but there was no way Paige could know that.

Framed in the brilliant sunlight from the sliding door, she glowed with energy. What would it be like to wake up every day with Paige smiling down at him?

Shaking the pointless wondering from his mind, Nick got to his feet and stretched to bring himself back to reality.

"I'll jump in the shower, then we can get going."

She stood, shifting the pages back to where they'd been before she sat down. The thoughtfulness of that simple gesture touched him deeply. Not only had she noticed where they came in sequence, she cared enough to put them back for him. He was still trying to get over that when she turned worried eyes on him.

"Nick, you need to get some sleep."

"I promised to show you around. Remember, hike up the falls? Swim with the dolphins?"

"Tell you what." Her hand on his jaw, she kissed his other cheek. "We can do all that tomorrow. You must be exhausted."

Her smile made him think of the dawn coming over the horizon to kiss the beach. He must be more tired than he thought. He was thinking like a poet instead of a P.I.

"Nothing a shower and some coffee won't cure," he lied smoothly. "Don't worry about me. I pull lots of all-nighters."

"Is that how you write so many books?"

He chuckled, ticking her nose. "There you go, uncovering my secrets again. Five minutes, I'll be ready to go."

He was rooting around in the dresser when she quietly said his name. Nick looked over his shoulder at her. "Yeah?"

"I wish you wouldn't write so many books."

After giving him a sad smile, she went onto the balcony. Puzzled, he stared after her. What a strange thing to wish for.

"Hey, get your own girl," Nick scolded the amorous bottle-nosed dolphin, giving it a light tap on the snout. Slapping its tail, the cheeky fish splashed him and leapt into the air with a series of triumphant squeaks.

"He kissed me!" Paige's eyes sparkled with delight as her hand went to her cheek. "Did you get it?"

"Right here." He grinned, holding up the waterproof single-use camera. "I got half a dozen shots, so you'll have plenty of pictures."

Three dolphins were vying for her attention, and she generously petted them all as they flashed by her.

When a fourth tried to flip Nick over, Paige laughed. "That one's female."

"Think so?"

"Definitely. She has very good taste."

"Aw, shucks." Nick grinned again. He'd had a smile planted on his face all day. Seeing Ocho Rios with her was even more fun than he'd imagined, and he had a pretty good imagination.

Their group started moving out of the water, and Paige quickly hugged each dolphin before taking Nick's hand to walk onto the beach. As they passed a souvenir stand, her head whipped around in a feminine gesture he knew all too well.

"Something catch your eye, Paige?"

He figured it was the pucha shell necklace with the dolphin charm that had gotten her attention. But she reached past it for a sterling silver rope chain.

"What do you think?" she asked, holding it up.

"It's really nice. A little heavy for you, though."

"Oh, it's not for me."

"I'm sure your dad will like it."

Nick knew he was prying, but his curiosity had gotten the better of him. He was fairly certain Paige didn't have a boyfriend but, if she did, it would be easier to put her out of his mind when he got home. Not easy, but easier.

"It's not for my dad, either."

Just what he wanted to hear. But he had his wallet out already, and he pulled out enough to pay for the choker.

"I can buy my own necklace, thank you."

"Okay." He wasn't keen on buying anything for her boyfriend, anyway.

Paige thanked the woman and opened the clasp on the choker. Then she turned to Nick and reached up to fasten it around his neck. Having her slender frame pressed against him for that fleeting moment felt perfect. He wanted to wrap his arms around her, keep her there. But if he did that, he'd never let her go, so he forced his hands to settle at her waist.

"For me?" he asked, trying to sound casual while his heart did barrel rolls.

She lightly kissed his lips, her eyes shining up at him. "Today was awesome, Nick." She traced the choker, her feathery touch searing his damp skin. "I hope this will remind you how much fun we had."

"I don't need a necklace for that, but thank you."

"You're welcome."

"Excuse me." The woman behind her at the ice cream bar tapped her shoulder, and Paige turned. "Isn't that Nick Stafford you're all cozied up with?"

Paige glanced over at Nick. He was stretched out on his stomach with his head on his arms, sound asleep. Two hours ago, he'd thrown himself onto that chaise and hadn't moved since. "No. Looks like him, though, doesn't he?"

The woman took another long look. "He's a dead ringer, that's for sure."

"Yeah. He gets that all the time."

Paige built a butterscotch sundae with plenty of syrup and whipped cream. As she sat down in her deck chair, she heard the low rumble of Nick's amusement. "Thanks, sweetheart. You're the best."

"You're welcome. I got a butterscotch sundae. Want some?"

She held out a spoonful, waving it under his nose. He opened one eye, then lifted his head, mouth wide open. "Mmm, that's good. Wake me in an hour for some more."

"I bet you say that to all the girls." She couldn't believe she just said that, but he laughed.

"Only the ones I really like."

"You like me best, though, right?"

When he didn't answer, she tipped the sundae dish and trailed melted ice cream down his bare back.

His eyes narrowed into a blistering glare. "I'm gonna have to get you for that."

Before she could react, he grabbed her and jumped into the nearest pool, which happened to be a lot cooler than she liked.

Sputtering, she swiped water out of her face and squirmed to get free.

"Okay, we're even. Now turn me loose. It's freezing in here."

He held onto her, clearly pleased with his childish stunt. "Payback's a bitch, ain't it, babe?"

She hushed him, scanning the pool area. "There might be kids out here."

"Sweet, thoughtful Paige." He held her face in his hands, gazing down at her intently.

Please, please, please, she begged silently. *Kiss me.*

He did. On the cheek. Then he let her go and, with a playful splash of water, he was gone.

"Nick?"

Struggling with a compound sentence, he glowered at the stubborn words. "Hmm?"

"Can I ask you something really, really personal?"

His gaze went to the doorway where Paige stood watching him. "Shoot."

"It's about your ex-wives."

"What about 'em?"

"What were they like? If you don't mind telling me."

He chuckled. "Why not? I've told you everything else. Let's see, I met Cammie in a psych class, sophomore year. She was a Trojans cheerleader."

Paige clicked her tongue. "Figures. What does Cammie stand for?"

"Camaro. I'm sure you can figure out why."

"California folks," she muttered, rolling her eyes.

He laughed. It was easy to laugh when he talked about

Cam. She'd made him so happy, he couldn't stand himself. Of course, back then it was easy. Make love in the morning before work, grind out a day at the marketing firm he despised, then race home and make love in the back hall, the kitchen, wherever. They honestly loved each other but, after five years, he realized he couldn't give her the life she wanted. The stable job with predictable hours, the house full of kids. She deserved those things, and he let her go so she could find them.

"She sounds nice. What about wife number two?"

He felt the tension traveling down his body and made a conscious effort to relax. From her sudden frown, he knew he'd failed. She crossed the sitting area and sat beside him on the love seat.

"Nick, I didn't mean to upset you. You don't have to tell me."

"It's not a nice story. It doesn't have a happy ending."

"Life's like that sometimes."

"Yeah, well, Joanna," he gritted the name between his teeth. "Joanna broke me."

"Broke you? How?"

"I met her at a party. I don't even remember where. All I remember was walking through the door and seeing her. She was the most beautiful woman I'd ever met, and she had no clue who I was." He rubbed his neck with a wry chuckle. "At least, that's what I thought. Later, I found out she'd read every one of my books and did a Dun and Bradstreet on me before our first date."

"Bitch."

Paige spat out the word venomously, eyes flaring with temper. For some reason, her violent reaction soothed him. She was furious with the woman who'd hacked him down and stripped him bare. Nick had endured the humiliation on his own, refusing to generate more publicity and feed Joanna's incessant need for attention.

If he'd known Paige back then, she would have stood by him. Somehow, knowing that made his past easier to deal with.

"It gets better. I came home early from a trip."

"Oh, Nick."

He grimaced. "Yup. Walked in on her and my publicist."

"How could he do that to you?"

"That's the kicker. My publicist was a woman."

Her jaw dropped, and he met her astonishment with a derisive laugh. "I married a lesbian, and I was so crazy about her, I didn't know it for two years. The only time she told me the truth was when she said she didn't love me."

The sharp edge on his voice cut his own ears, but to her credit, Paige never blinked. "Then what happened?"

"She shredded me. Neglect, emotional abuse, the works. I was working, traveling a lot and, for the most part, it was her word against mine. California's a community property state, but she graciously offered to accept ten thousand a month."

"Dollars?"

Nick smiled. Even if Paige truly hated somebody, she'd never try to destroy him. "Yeah. We settled on an astronomical lump sum, and she got the house besides, but at least I don't have to write her a check every month."

"Then it was worth it," she declared staunchly. "What did you do after that?"

"Moved out to Malibu, bought a place that was mine. A place I didn't have to share with anybody."

"What about the women you date? Don't you take them there?"

"Sure, for the night, or the weekend." He caught himself and pointed at her with a mock glare. "I never tell people stuff like that. You're *way* too easy to talk to."

"So, now you trust me."

It wasn't a question. It was a quiet observation, and Nick couldn't help smiling at her. "Yeah, I do."

"How does it feel?"

"Good." She opened her mouth, and he stopped her with a finger over her lips. "But before you start lecturing me, I'd like to say you're different."

She moved his hand away, weaving her fingers through his. "Nick, I'm like everybody else. If you'd let somebody close enough to see who you really are, you could be so happy."

"You mean a woman."

"Of course, I mean a woman. Don't you want more than this?" Indicating the empty suite, she added, "Don't you want someone to love, to share your life with?"

"Right now, I don't have a life fit to share. It's still in pieces, and I don't know where most of them are." He paused to smile at her. "You helped me find some of them, these last few days. Thank you."

"You're welcome." She kissed his cheek before curling up to read his latest pages. "I'm glad I could help."

She had, more than she'd ever know. And he knew the perfect way to show her how much it meant to him.

Chapter Four

"**W**here have you been?" Paige asked as Nick hustled into the dining room. "I thought you ditched me."

"Forgot something in my room." He kissed her cheek before pulling the other chair around to sit next to her. Not across from her, the way he usually did. Judging by his eagerness, she was in for a surprise.

"Nick, what did you do?"

"Close your eyes."

"Why?" she asked, suspicious and excited all at once.

"Just close your eyes."

When she did, Paige felt something cool slipping onto her wrist, followed by the little clicks of a clasp. "Okay, you can open 'em."

As she ran her finger around the ring of dolphins, Paige couldn't quite believe it was hers. He bought the bracelet for her because he thought it would make her happy. In a way, it did. It also made her very, very sad. She didn't want gifts, pretty jewelry and such.

She wanted him. But that, as he'd so clearly stated, he couldn't give her.

"It's beautiful. Thank you." Her voice came in a shaky whisper.

"I'm glad you like it." Then he took her hand and kissed it, his eyes twinkling at her.

He was so much more than she'd expected. She'd known he was talented and handsome, but he was also attentive and caring, grateful for every kindness he received. He'd come to Jamaica to escape the craziness of his life and instead gave her the excitement she'd been craving.

He'd opened up his closely guarded private life, telling her things other people didn't know. Sharing himself, giving her glimpses into the depths of him. But this was their last night together. She was flying home in the morning, and she'd never see him again. She'd known that all along, but suddenly it was unbearable.

Paige wrenched her hand away, left the table and fled through the double doors onto the wide deck. She was dangerously close to tears, and she didn't want Nick to remember her bawling like a spoiled child. Gripping the rail tightly, she pulled salt air into her lungs. She *would not* cry.

She heard a polite "Thank you," and turned to see Nick holding the door for an elderly couple. With a deep breath, she stiffened her spine and plastered a smile on her face.

"Are you all right?" he asked, obviously concerned by her bizarre reaction to his generous gift.

"I'm fine. It's just really warm in there, and I got a little dizzy. The breeze off the ocean fixed me right up."

"Are you sure?" When she nodded, he offered her his hand. "Walk with me?"

"Okay." She slipped off her sandals and hooked her fingers in the leather straps before taking his hand. A moonlit stroll on the beach with Nick Stafford. She'd kill the person who woke her from this dream.

"Paige, I'm sorry. I wanted to surprise you."

"You did that, all right." She managed a shaky laugh, looking out over the water to avoid his perceptive gaze. "Look, there's the first star. You should make a wish."

"I wish you'd tell me what's wrong."

She couldn't look at him, so she kept her eyes on the star.

"If it's not about the bracelet, what is it?"

She sighed and turned to him. She couldn't let him go on thinking he'd done something to upset her. "I'm just not feeling very well."

The time-honored lady's excuse. Of course, that was because it worked.

He swallowed it easily, pressing the back of his hand to her cheek. "You're a little warm."

"Too much sun, I guess. I'm sure I'll feel better tomorrow."

"You're leaving tomorrow." He hadn't meant to say it, but the words slipped out before he could stop them.

"I know," she whispered, her eyes filling with tears.

A crazy idea pushed up from the back of his mind. "Do you think you could you stay one more day?"

Excitement illuminated her features, then dimmed as she slowly shook her head. "My plane ticket's for tomorrow."

"So we'll change it. No big deal." He reached into his jacket pocket for his cell phone and handed it to her.

She cocked her head and smiled. "I'd really love to stay."

"I'd really love to have you stay." Somehow, his arms had found their way around her waist. "I could beg if you want."

"No, that's—how?"

It was easy to match her saucy grin. "Oh, I don't know," he murmured, kissing along the curve of her shoulder. "I'll think of something."

She giggled when he hit a ticklish spot, looking up at him with a playful glint in her eyes. "I'm not convinced yet."

Nick waited for reason to kick in and remind him not to go where she was leading him.

It never did.

Very cautiously, he leaned in and kissed her. He gathered her into his arms, deepening the kiss because he couldn't help himself. His phone thudded into the sand as she wrapped her arms around his back and pulled him even closer. God help him, he let her do it.

He'd known all along this would happen. A little of Paige would never be enough. He wanted all of her, the way he'd imagined that first night.

But he couldn't give her the same.

The stark truth hit him hard, and he grasped her shoulders to force himself away from her. "Paige, I'm sorry. That was way out of line."

"I liked it. Very much."

She didn't try to hold him, but he couldn't move more than a step away. When she smiled at him, his heart rolled over like a love-struck puppy. For several long, uncomfortable moments, he endured her probing gaze. He felt it burrowing deep inside him, bringing light to places that had been dark until she opened them again.

"I know you think no one will want you because you're broken," she said softly. "But you're wrong."

"Maybe you're wrong."

She silenced him with a gentle finger on his lips, and he fought back a sigh. Every time she touched him, he could feel his battered heart reaching for her. She was dangerously close, but he just couldn't keep her at bay anymore.

"Nick, will you do something for me?"

Dazed beyond coherent speech, he nodded.

"I want you to trust yourself again."

"You don't know what you're asking."

She leveled him with the most tender kiss he'd ever gotten. "For me?"

With her eyes shining into his, he gave her the only honest answer he could.

"I'll try."

It was after three when Nick rolled over and noticed Paige's lights were still on. He walked over to the open door and smiled at what he saw. She was curled up, sound asleep, his new novel propped open against her knees.

He laid the book on her bedside table, then pulled the covers over her. Gazing down at her, an odd feeling swelled in his chest. She'd caught him by surprise, this sweet, wonderful woman who saw so much hidden away inside him. She could so easily become his lover, but he wanted more for her.

She deserved to have all the things he saw dancing in her eyes when she looked at him, and he couldn't give them to her. He didn't have them to give.

With a quiet sigh, he reached over and turned off the lamp. Pale moonlight splashed over her peaceful face and, leaning down, he brushed his lips across her cheek.

"Sweet dreams, Paige."

Chapter Five

"Y ou're quiet this morning," Nick observed while Paige shoved eggs Benedict around her plate. "Sleep okay?"

She shrugged, then gave up on the eggs and sipped her orange juice.

"I wished you sweet dreams. Didn't it work?"

"You did?" She was amazed, convinced he'd given up on dreams a long time ago. "That was real nice of you. But no, it didn't work."

He took a sip of his coffee and set the cup back in its saucer. "I was wondering if you have some spare time coming up."

Her heart leapt joyfully, but she kept her expression calm. "I could make time. What did you have in mind?"

"Well, this new book's pretty different from what I've done before. I've been thinking I should have somebody read the manuscript for me."

"That sounds like a good idea."

"I thought maybe you'd like to take a stab at it. It'd be a lot of work, and I'm not sure what readers make."

"Oh, I'd do it for nothing." She barely suppressed the urge to clap her hands.

"One thing you're gonna have to learn, sweetheart." He leaned toward her, like he was sharing the secrets of the universe. "Don't ever say you'll do something for nothing. They'll take you up on it."

She folded her arms in disapproval. "How did you get to be so cynical?"

"Practice." Nick grinned down at the orange he was peeling. "So, would you like to read it or not?"

"I'd love to." She smiled. "When?"

"At the rate I'm going, late spring, maybe."

Her smile faded, replaced by worry. "Nick, you'll kill yourself. Why do you work so hard?"

"That's what I do. Well, that and surf."

"I think you should surf more."

A brilliant idea jumped into his head, and he grinned. "I could teach you, if you want."

"No." Shaking her head firmly, she waved her hands. "I'm a klutz on land. I'd be a disaster on a surfboard."

He kept peeling his orange, waiting for her innate curiosity to change her mind.

After a few seconds, she asked, "Is it hard?"

"Surfing? Nope. Especially here. The waves are smaller than in California. Jamaica's a good place to learn."

Out of the corner of his eye, he saw her glance out at the water rolling lazily onto the beach. She was so cute, torn between her good sense and her sense of adventure.

"Paige." When she looked toward him, he smiled reassurance. "I promise you'll be fine. I won't let anything happen to you."

After a deep breath, she nodded. "Okay. After breakfast, I'll watch you. Then maybe," she pointed at him, "*maybe* I'll try it."

"Sure, whatever."

"Don't you dare laugh at me."

"I'm not."

"Yes, you are. Inside, you're laughing like a maniac."

How she knew that, he had no clue, but he wasn't surprised.

Nick managed to get cleared through to the Delta wing of the airport. One of the managers recognized him and scooted him through the back corridors like he was the president. After signing the guy's name tag and swearing five times not to tell anybody, Nick emerged at the gate where Paige sat waiting for her plane.

She was folded up in a chair, her face buried in the sleeves of her Carolina Panthers sweatshirt. For the first time in his career, Nick walked past people eagerly approaching him.

He dropped to his knees in front of Paige and took her hands. When she raised her head, the sight of her tear-streaked face was the end of him. Gathering her into his arms, he felt every sob tear through his heart.

Very literally, he didn't think he could let her go. When the boarding call for her flight came over the speakers, she lifted her head from his shoulder, wiping her wet cheeks with the ribbed cuff of her sweatshirt.

"You'll hurt yourself doing it like that." He brushed her tears away with his thumbs. Her mouth trembled, and he gently kissed one corner, then the other. Throwing aside what was left of his caution, he lingered for a deep kiss. Her ragged sigh was absolute torture, and it took all his strength to pull away from her.

Nick smoothed damp curls back from her face and dredged up a smile. "I'm out East all the time. I'll be there again soon.

I'll bring that manuscript for you. Maybe after you read it, you can come up with a title."

With a deep breath, she nodded and gave him a brave smile. "Okay."

He stood with her, picking up her carry-on to hand it to her. She hefted the bag onto her shoulder and slipped her arms around his waist. "Remember what I said the other night."

"What exactly was that again?"

She rolled her eyes and lightly smacked his cheek. "About trusting yourself. Don't forget, now."

"I won't," he promised, resting his hand over hers. Turning his head, he kissed her smooth palm, savoring that last touch of her skin. "Safe trip, Paige."

"You, too. 'Bye, Nick."

Several times, she turned to look back, as if she couldn't bear to leave him. He kept his eyes on her while she walked up the gangway and turned the corner. Then he stood at the window, watching her plane taxi onto the runway and lift into the clouds. He pressed his forehead to the glass as a bone-chilling ache settled in his chest.

Desolate.

He knew what it meant.

Now he knew how it felt.

Chapter Six

Nick came in from his morning run on the beach and saw the blinking light on his answering machine. Anita sounded a little breathless. Calling from her treadmill, no doubt. That meant she was jazzed about the pages he'd faxed her.

"I thought I told you to take a vacation," she scolded him. Then she laughed. "Nick, this stuff is fantastic. When I got to the whirlpool scene, I needed ice. You've been holding out on me all these years. Who knew you could write such great sex? Anyway, whatever you're doing and whoever you're doing it with, keep it up. Send me more when you have it. Don't leave me hanging too long."

"Don't worry," Nick grumbled as he reached in the refrigerator for a bottle of water.

He headed for his study, where the computer had been humming almost constantly for three days. His e-mail alert was playing, and he clicked the mailbox icon. His heart surged when he saw the address.

"Thought you'd like these," Paige's message said, a little

star over the *i* in her signature. The attachments were pictures from Jamaica.

He saved the files and shoved photo paper into the printer, clicking the print command. While he waited, he monkeyed with a shot of her from their last dinner together, cropping and framing it to be his new screen saver.

Leaning back in his chair, he stared at the image that had become his inspiration for the first heroine he'd ever written. Ellen Charles, the woman who crashed into Derek at Heathrow Airport and disappeared into the crowd. It took him a hundred pages to find her again, but when he did, it was magic.

Lost in warm memories of Paige, Nick's mind wandered, taking his heart with it. Some of his heart, at least.

The rest of it was in Charleston.

"Well, look at you," Brenda crowed when Paige walked in for work.

"Do you like it?" She was still a little hesitant about the flirty lavender dress. It covered what it was supposed to cover, and the salesgirl had convinced her it looked perfect with the strappy ivory heels. But it was far from her usual style, and she'd come close to leaving it in her closet.

"I love it. That color is great on you. How was Jamaica?"

"Fabulous. The food was incredible, and we had great weather. Thanks for rearranging my schedule so I could stay longer."

"No problem." Brenda lifted Paige's hand, whistling her approval of the dolphin bracelet. "Very nice. And expensive, I bet. Who gave it to you?"

Before Paige could respond, a massive bouquet of white roses bobbed in the front door and wound their way over to the register.

"Paige?" The deliveryman sounded like George Harriman, but she couldn't see him behind the roses.

"What?"

"These are for you." He set the vase on the counter and winked at her. "Must've been some vacation. No card, though. He just laughed and said you'd know who they're from."

"Thanks for bringing them, George." Paige opened her new purse to get him a tip, but he held up his hands.

"Taken care of, believe you me. Whoever this dude is, he knows how to thank folks. Funny accent, though. He's not from around here."

"Can I see your fishing license, please?"

"Come on, darlin'," he drawled, leaning on the counter. "Just in case I wanted to check up on him, how far would I have to go?"

Paige plucked a rose from the vase and held it to her nose, drinking in the rich scent. "California."

"Well, now." He grinned. "Big time stud material, is he?"

"Mmm-hmm."

George's dark eyes twinkled at her. "I like your outfit."

"Thank you." Paige fought off an instinctive blush and smiled at him instead. All through high school, he'd never looked at her twice. Her sudden change in status was flattering.

"Go on, get outta here before you scare off all my customers." Brenda shooed him out, the gleam in her eyes making it clear she planned on continuing her interrogation.

For the first time in years, Paige beat her to the punch. "Before you ask me, I'm not talking about him. He's real nice, and I like him a lot, and that's all I'm saying."

"Honey, that's a hundred dollars' worth of roses if it's a penny. You don't wanna talk about him, fine." She pointed to the elegant bouquet. "But those are worth a thousand words."

As Brenda walked off, Paige decided her boss was right. And unless she missed her guess, she'd hear at least a thousand words about those roses before the day was out.

"Excuse me." The very well-dressed woman smiled and extended a manicured hand across the counter. "Are you Paige Ramsey?"

Paige shook her hand, perplexed. "Yes. Can I help you?"

"The Paige Ramsey who just spent the week in—let me see." The reporter checked her PDA. "Jamaica?"

When Paige nodded, the woman smiled again and handed her a business card. Janice Hawthorne, *Entertainment Beat*.

Then Janice asked, "Have you talked to anyone else yet?"

"About what?"

"About what?" she echoed, laughing politely as she put a hand on Brenda's shoulder. "Oh, she's good. You must love working with her, Ms.—?"

"Ames. What's going on?"

"I just wanted to catch Ms. Ramsey before things get hectic, make sure I get an exclusive."

Paige had lost her patience, and she let out an exasperated sigh. "For *what*?"

"Great," Janice muttered with a scowl. "Those West Coast vultures scooped me."

Following her gaze, Paige looked toward the suspended television and saw the opening story on a daily entertainment show. She couldn't hear the commentary, but the picture on the screen told her everything. Nick and her kissing on the beach, silhouetted by a sky full of stars. The caption read *Star-crossed Lovers*.

"Nick Stafford?" Brenda asked in a squeaky whisper. "You went to Jamaica with Nick Stafford?"

"Of course not. I never even met him until that book signing."

Brenda zeroed in on the dolphins circling Paige's wrist. "He bought you that bracelet, didn't he?"

"You two met at a book signing?" Janice asked, her stylus flying across the screen of her PDA. "He bought you jewelry?"

Reason finally kicked in, and Paige folded her arms, clamping her mouth shut. "Ms. Hawthorne, I'm not discussing Nick Stafford with you." She shot Brenda a lethal glare. "Or anybody else."

A feral gleam came into the reporter's dark eyes, and she took an envelope from her slim briefcase. "A thousand dollars, Ms. Ramsey. For fifteen minutes of your time."

After eight rings, Nick finally figured out how to turn on the phone. "What?" he muttered, focusing bleary eyes on the clock beside his bed. Must be a nightmare. He'd been asleep for all of forty-five minutes.

"Oh, Nick, I'm sorry. I forgot how early it is there. I just didn't know what else to do."

"Paige?" He bolted upright in response to her frantic tone. "What's wrong?"

"Everything. Do you know Janice Hawthorne from *Entertainment Beat*?"

"Sure."

"How about Paul Ferguson? Joseph Cardinale?"

"Yeah, I know 'em." Nick yawned, pulling a pillow up behind his back. "Why?"

Paige filled him in on her eventful morning, her voice continuing to rise in pitch and frustration. Nick flipped the TV to the entertainment channel, groaning at the pictures of them together. By the pool, at dinner, in the casino, under the stars. Somebody was happy this morning. That kiss had dollar signs written all over it.

"It was a guest at the hotel, sweetheart," he assured her, clicking the TV off. "This happens all the time. People take pictures, then sell them to the highest bidder. Don't worry about it."

"Easy for you to say. You live in Malibu, and nobody can get near you. I've got reporters coming to work, waving money in my face."

"Really? How much?"

He chuckled, pleased to hear her laugh. Then she got serious again.

"Nick, what do you want me to do?"

"Whatever you want. This is your chance to be famous. You said you wanted some excitement in your life."

A shaky breath came over the line, and when she spoke, he heard tears. "I'd rather die of boredom than cause trouble for you. But I don't know what Brenda told that reporter."

"Who's Brenda?"

"My boss. She has a big mouth. Janice Hawthorne knows how we met, and Brenda made a big deal about my bracelet in front of her."

She was wearing the bracelet he bought her. Knowing that made his chest swell with male pride. Then he turned his attention to the problem at hand. "What did Janice say?"

"With you finishing your book tour in Charleston, she thinks you set things up to meet me in Jamaica. She wouldn't believe me when I said you didn't."

"Not with my reputation." Fully awake now, he glanced at the clock again. "Look, it's too early for me to call Anita, but I will. Maybe she can do some damage control, but I doubt it. If they found you already, they're way ahead of her. She doesn't even know about you."

Yet, he added silently. Because she'd grill him worse than the CIA, making sure the newshounds didn't know anything she couldn't spin, exploit, or flat out deny.

"What should I do in the meantime?"

"You have to decide what you're comfortable with. It's your call."

"I'm not talking to them."

There was no hesitation in her determined tone, and he knew she'd hold her ground. Paige Ramsey might be the epitome of a soft-spoken Southern rose, but she had a lot of spunk.

Which was why he'd fallen in love with her.

He looked at the picture in the floating frame on his bedside table. Paige with her dolphin admirer. He could almost hear her laughing.

God, he missed her. He kept waiting for it to fade, but every day he missed her more.

"I'll get back to you after I call Anita," he promised.

"Okay. I'm sorry to start your day like this."

"Don't worry about it, Paige. Besides, now I have something to look forward to."

"Oh, really? What's that?"

"Talking to you later." The line hummed quietly, and he grinned. "Tell me you're smiling."

"I'm smiling." But her voice was oddly flat, and he decided she must be more upset than she was letting on.

He lowered his voice to a throaty growl. "What're you wearing, babe?"

She rewarded him with the laugh he was after. Then he got something he hadn't expected. "I really miss you, Nick. I wish—"

His heart rolled over helplessly. "You wish what?" *Ask me*, he added silently, *and it's yours*.

Suddenly, her voice was terse. "I have to go. I'll get that information from you later."

The line clicked as she hung up. He switched off the handset and rested it against his forehead with a sigh. It was six o'clock. Anita wouldn't be coherent for at least two hours. More than enough time to plot out Derek's fight in the alley.

Anita found him on the beach, gazing out toward the white-capped waves at something only he could see. Taking her digital camera from her bag, she snapped a few pictures before she could feel guilty about it. She scribbled the words *lost in thought* on a business card and tucked it in with the camera.

She'd been an agent for twelve years, and Nick Stafford was the most fiercely private person she'd ever represented. A charming California boy, he possessed a quick wit and a bone-melting grin. That, and the information in his bio, was all anybody really knew about him. The other day, in the chapters he'd faxed her, she'd gotten a glimpse of something else.

Yearning, she'd thought as she read the first few pages. Further on, she saw unquenchable desire. Then she got to the scene in the whirlpool. The sequence was so steamy, she read it four times, amazed that he could write such pulsing, romantic sex.

Once he finished the book, they'd leak some key excerpts a couple of months ahead of its official release date. With the advance publicity and pre-order campaign she'd already planned, the booksellers wouldn't be able to keep up with demand.

They'd put the pose she'd just captured on the back cover, and his new book would outsell the rest of the series combined. Then it would be time for a new publishing contract.

Ignoring the sand and the wreck it would make of her brand-new Versaci suit, Anita plunked herself down next to him, trying to remember why she'd come out there in the first place. Oh, right, the magazines. The show biz channels. Priceless free publicity for her favorite client. Every agent's dream.

"So," she began casually, enjoying the breeze as it ruffled her hair. "You kissed Scarlett O'Hara and somebody got pictures." He turned to her with a wry look. "Anything else I should know?"

"Nope." He focused back on the ocean.

"Nick, there's nothing out there. What are you looking at?"

"You know, there must be a point where the Pacific and Atlantic oceans meet."

Bewildered by his comment, Anita blinked. But he wasn't looking at her, so her confusion didn't make much of an impression on him. "I guess. I never thought about it."

"Down around Australia," he continued as if she hadn't spoken. He crossed his arms on his bent knees and dropped his chin there. "They must come together somewhere."

His voice had gone kind of dreamy, and the trouble siren in Anita's head was wailing full blast. Without thinking, she brushed the hair back from his deeply shadowed eyes. He looked exhausted. More than that, he looked sad. "What's going on?"

He buried his face in his arms, but she couldn't miss his heavy sigh. "I've got another chapter for you."

"What?" Vague worry blossomed into fear. "You're months from any kind of a deadline. You'll wear yourself out working like this."

She knelt in front of him and brought his head up. When he stubbornly kept his eyes from hers, she lightly tapped his cheek. "Look at me."

That got her a sizzling glare, but at least she had his full attention. "Does this have anything to do with Scarlett?"

"Paige." He smiled, as if just saying it made him feel better. "Her name is Paige."

"Right. Paige Ramsey. I remember. The one who's telling all the reporters where to shove their notebooks."

With a chuckle, he dragged his hands through his hair. "Yeah, that's her."

Anita knew better than to blurt out the question on the tip of her tongue. She was dying for details on this mysterious beachcomber, but her usual direct approach wouldn't get her anywhere, so she tried the subtle thing. "Do you want to tell me about her?"

"She misses me."

Chapter Seven

"**D**on't they know what star-crossed means?" Brenda complained as they stocked the shelves with the latest gossip magazines. "It means they never get together."

Paige didn't respond. She was so tired it took all her concentration not to mix the new *Sports Illustrated* in with *Sports Fishing*.

Brenda held up one of the glossy rags. "You two look incredible together. Don't tell me all this doesn't bother you."

Actually, it had at first, but it paled next to missing Nick. When she let herself think about how far away he was, her eyes filled with tears. The way they were doing now.

"Oh, honey, I'm sorry." Brenda put an arm around Paige's shoulders in a comforting hug. "This must be awful for you, having these reporters around all the time."

"It's not that." She twirled the sparkling dolphins around her wrist. Much as she liked it, she had to stop wearing the bracelet. It reminded her too vividly of Nick. "We don't just look good together. We *are* good together."

"You're really crazy about him, aren't you?"

Paige nodded miserably.

"Did you tell him?"

When she sniffled and shook her head, Brenda demanded, "Why not?"

"I wanted to, but he said we should just be friends."

From behind her, she heard a tired, apologetic voice. "He was wrong."

Astonished, she looked over her shoulder and saw Nick, dressed in faded jeans and a USC sweatshirt. He looked four steps past exhausted. When he held his arms open, she launched herself into them, burying her face in his chest.

"I can't believe you're here," she whispered as his arms came around her. It felt wonderful. Then she realized it wasn't even nine o'clock, and she lifted her head to gape at him. "When did you leave California?"

"Twenty-six hundred miles ago."

"Oh, my God," Brenda murmured in an awed voice. "He knows how far it is."

With his practiced grin, Nick held out his hand. "You must be Brenda."

"I must be." She giggled, then motioned to the magazines on the end cap. "I think some of this is my fault. I'm real sorry."

"Don't worry about it." His attention went back to Paige, and he smoothed an unruly ringlet back behind her ear. "How're you holding up, sweetheart?"

Brenda sighed. "Oh, I love that." When Paige glared at her, she added, "You know, I really should go clean up the front counter. Excuse me."

"Nice meeting you, Brenda."

Since he'd come through the door, he hadn't taken his eyes from Paige. She looked worn out, and he could swear she'd lost weight in the few days since he'd last seen her. He'd never quite understood how a woman could appear fragile. Now he did. She made him think of a china doll, all the more precious because she could be broken.

"I managed to find your house, but you were already gone. That's quite a crew you've got out there."

"They destroyed my rose bushes."

For the first time in days, Nick laughed. He couldn't help it, even while she scowled at him.

"If that's your only complaint, I'll buy you a hundred rose bushes." Then he ran a finger over the deep circles under her eyes, down the accentuated hollows of her cheeks. "But what brought these on?"

"I miss you."

She'd told him that over the phone, but seeing the tears shining in her eyes as she said those incredible words made them more believable.

"Do you know how many times a day I turn to say something to you, and you're not there?" She shook her head, and he gently kissed her. "Too many to count, and it kills me every time. I miss the way you look at me, the way you say my name. On the way here from the airport, I heard that in a song on the radio."

She smiled shyly, fingering the gold garland of leaves embroidered on his sweatshirt. "I love that song."

"I thought it sounded like your kind of music." He put an arm around her shoulders and headed for the door. "They play a lot of country around here?"

"Yeah." She laughed and, in an exaggerated Carolina accent reminded him, "You're in the South now, boy."

He leaned back against the white Mercedes and gathered her into his arms. "I gotta get me one o' them accents."

"Nick, why are you here?"

"Missed you." He kissed her, longer than he should have

considering they were on the street. "A lot."

"You came all this way because you missed me?"

"Actually, I came all this way because *you* missed *me*. You don't mind, don't you?"

Her lips trembled with a smile. A tear started down her cheek, and he caught it with his knuckle, kissing the moist trail it left on her skin.

"Look, I know you're working, so I'm gonna go crash for a while. When are you done?"

"Four. The reporters are usually gone by seven. I could make you dinner, if you want."

"I'll be there." Nick slipped his arms around her waist and smiled down at her. The ivory scoop-neck sweater and Black Watch kilt looked new. "Did I tell you I like your outfit?"

"No."

"Well, I do. Very much." Tracing the outline of her lips, he warned her, "If I kiss you again, it'll be news in ten minutes."

"I don't care."

Nick drove down the narrow lane and shook his head at the cars and vans parked opposite Paige's beach house. A few calls from Anita had at least gotten them out of the front yard. He pulled into the driveway and parked behind Paige's silver Escort.

He sauntered down the row of vehicles, stopping at open windows to chat with the various entertainment reporters. They were heading out in a day or two, they all assured him. In return, he told them he'd broken things off with Amity Farrell. It wouldn't be news to her, since she was in Bimini with the Raiders' new quarterback, but the newshounds were thrilled with the bone. His good deed for the day.

As Nick followed the brick path to the front porch, he surveyed the wreck of Paige's yard. Before he left, he'd arrange for a landscaper to come out in the spring and replant everything.

Through the front door he could hear Paige singing along with a pretty country ballad on the radio. When he knocked, she came around the corner into the small foyer.

She dried her hands on a towel and opened the door for him. "Come on in. I see you made it through the net."

"Yeah. They're all afraid of Anita. Mention her name, they run for cover."

Nick stepped into a small living room dominated by floor-to-ceiling shelves full of books. "Whoa. I thought *I* had a lot of books."

They were all in alphabetical order by author. Nick found his books on the shelf beside an impressive collection of Nora Roberts. When he opened *Stitch in Time*, his first Foster book, he was surprised to see his signature. "Don't tell me I met you six years ago and forgot."

"No. I got it from your website. There's a thing where people can buy the book and tell you what name they want for the autograph."

"I know I came out here, though. That was my first trip to Charleston, and I loved it."

Paige returned the book to the shelf. "I didn't go."

"Too busy?"

"Too chicken. Just *thinking* about meeting you made me so nervous, I knew if I went I'd gush all over you and make a fool of myself."

Her hands were resting on the shelf, and Nick closed his over them. Standing behind her, he wrapped her in a warm embrace, and she sank back against him, as if she wanted to be in his arms as much as he wanted her there. "You weren't nervous this time?"

"I didn't say that." Still in his arms, she turned to face him. "I just decided it was worth it. I even practiced what I wanted to say. Then you smiled at me, and it went straight out of my head."

"Well, I'm glad you went. It gave us something to talk about later."

Her face lit up, and she grabbed his arms excitedly. "I just thought of a title for your book. How about *Time After Time*?"

"Perfect."

He lightly kissed her and pulled away, surprised when she brought his mouth back to hers. Her boldness caught him off guard. Passion bubbled dangerously close to the surface these days and, with one kiss, she'd unleashed it. He was willing to bet she had no clue what it took to get it tethered again.

Reluctantly, Nick grasped her shoulders and stepped back. Raking a hand through his hair, he sighed. "I'm a mess, sweetheart. Are you sure you want all this?"

She smiled again, kissing him on the cheek. "Oh, I'm a project person. We'll just call you a work in progress."

Slinging an arm around her shoulders, he chuckled as they walked into the kitchen.

"I've been called worse."

They were finishing their peach cobbler when Paige heard a muted version of *Satisfaction*.

"I think your pocket's ringing," she said, nodding toward the jacket hanging on the back door.

"It's probably my parents. I called them when I got here, but I had to leave a message. Excuse me a minute."

He took his phone into the living room, and she cleared the table. They'd had a nice, cozy dinner, full of light-hearted conversation. She easily pictured her life this way. If she turned out to be any good as a manuscript reader, she could actually help Nick with his writing.

Days with him would be wonderful, full of challenge and adventure. And the nights she could only imagine. It would be a refreshing change from the quiet existence she'd always known.

Besides, she loved him, and she knew he loved her. He just hadn't figured it out yet.

When he stalked into the kitchen, he didn't look very happy. "Just a minute, Mom." He held the phone out to Paige. "Please tell her I haven't gone around the bend."

"Why don't you handle her the way you did those reporters?"

"Come on, Paige. This is my mom. She's way tougher than the reporters."

She put the phone to her ear and smiled. "She said to tell you she heard that, Nicholas Charles. Yes, ma'am, he's rolling his eyes. Now he's banging his head against the wall. I think it's safe to say you embarrassed him. No, I won't smack him, but I'll tell him you wanted me to."

He snatched the phone back. "Okay now?" He listened for a minute, a little boy's grin slowly working its way across his face. "Yeah, she's great. I'll tell her. See you soon."

"My mother wants to meet you," he said as he picked up a towel to start drying the dishes in the rack.

"I'd like to meet her, too. She seems real nice."

"She is. Dad's fantastic, too." Nick set a dry glass in the open cupboard. "Forty-three years, and they're still crazy about each other. Can't put 'em in the back seat of a car."

"They sound wonderful."

"They are." He almost told her he wanted what they had, a lifetime with someone who saw his flaws and loved him anyway. Instead, he said, "In Jamaica you said you do stories with your niece. What do you write about?"

"We did one about a unicorn who lived under a rainbow." She stopped, smiling as she shook her head. "Never mind."

"No, tell me about it."

"It's full of dreams and wishes," she hedged, obviously convinced he'd hate it.

"Tell me."

The story was a typical fairy tale, but he liked hearing her soft drawl flow through what she was saying, seeing her eyes sparkle with the electrifying enthusiasm he so often felt but never saw.

No two ways about it. Crazy as it seemed, he was falling for a woman he'd known for ten days.

"Your turn."

Jerked out of his reverie, he had no clue what she meant. "What?"

"Tell me a story. One with a happy ending."

"I don't know. I've never done one of those."

She stepped closer, threading her fingers through his while she fixed him with a pleading look. "For me?"

"Okay, but I don't do princesses or knights in shining armor."

She rolled her eyes, and he laughed, spinning her around to pull her back against his chest. He loved having her with him, where he could touch her, hold her when he wanted to. Resting his chin on top of her head, he wove a tale with a heroine who talked to the stars and convinced the hero to believe in magic.

When he stopped, she waited a few seconds, then tipped her head back to give him a nice little pout. "That's it? I wanted a happy ending."

"She made him believe in magic. That was a major accomplishment, considering how dense he was."

"I guess." She turned to face him. "What happens next?"

"You tell me."

From her mischievous grin, he knew she'd figured out the story was about them.

"I think the heroine has to help the hero find his own magic.

Then he can talk to the stars, too."

"I think the hero would really like that." He smiled, toying with the soft curls on her shoulder. "He's not used to people trying so hard for him."

"She knows he's worth it," she said, resting her hand on his jaw. Studying him intently, she tilted her head. "What is it?"

Nick tried to swallow the lump in his throat before he answered. "When I'm with you, I feel," he paused, searching for a way to explain it. "I don't know. Unbroken, I guess."

"Is that a word?"

He chuckled. "No, but it's the best I can do."

"Then I guess we'll just have to find a way to spend more time together."

"I'll work on it," he replied, sealing his promise with a kiss.

Chapter Eight

"**B**renda, where are you taking me?"

With a hot pink bandanna over her eyes, Paige couldn't tamp down her excitement. They were driving somewhere on the highway. She could tell by the sound of cars whizzing by her open window. It was one of those beautiful early spring days that tease you with the promise of summertime.

"No peeking," Brenda ordered, turning sharply before parking the car. Paige heard her get out and then open the passenger door. "Careful, now, there's a puddle."

Paige let Brenda lead her a few steps, then stopped mid-stride. Those were planes. There could be only one reason she'd be at the airport in the middle of the week.

Nick. He'd been to Charleston twice since his first trip, each visit a surprise. Every time, he rented a different flashy car and drove to the store to pick her up after work. He said he got a kick out of seeing her jaw hit the floor when she looked up expecting a customer and saw him instead.

Paige ripped off her blindfold, her heart racing wildly. "Brenda, am I going to California?"

"Hmm, let me see." Brenda pulled an envelope out of her purse, laughing when Paige snatched it from her. "Nick sent it for you."

"This is awesome." Paige hugged her impulsively. "But I don't have a suitcase."

"Your mom packed one for you. I brought it earlier and left it in the holding room. By the way, you're not scheduled to work again until Monday."

"You're the best. Thank you."

While she checked in, Brenda waited on the far side of the terminal.

"Come on, Paige. Let's get something to eat."

"You don't have to wait with me. I'll be fine."

Her friend just smiled and pushed open the door to a small pub. It took Paige's eyes a moment to adjust to the dimly lit room. It wasn't very crowded, and she followed her friend to a table in the corner, the only one with a vase of gardenias.

"What's this?" she asked, eyes narrowing suspiciously. Brenda was way too quiet. She usually chattered non-stop.

"Why don't you read the card?"

Paige whirled and met up with a pair of twinkling blue eyes. From the delighted expression he was wearing, Nick was very pleased with his stunt. Laughing, she hugged him and then shook her head in confusion.

"I thought I was going to California."

"You are." He kissed her hand. "With me. It's a long, boring trip. I thought you'd like some company."

"You knew about this," Paige accused Brenda, who held up her hands.

"I'm just the chauffeur. Blame him."

Nick grinned again and motioned them to the booth. "Have a seat, ladies. Lunch is on me."

* * *

"That's L.A.?" Paige gawked at the expanse of convoluted highways that snaked around huge tracts of high-rise buildings.

"Yup. Something, huh?"

"I'll say. Where does everybody park?"

Nick laughed as he buckled his seatbelt. "Wherever they can."

"You don't live here, though."

"I did for a few years. It's fun, and there's always something to do."

Leaning her elbow on the armrest between their seats, she propped her chin on her hand. "Like what?"

"Parties, restaurants, clubs." He shrugged dismissively. "Every kind of networking you could think of. One weekend, a friend of mine invited me out to his dad's condo at Malibu. You know, drink, surf, rate the bikinis."

"Hmm."

"Anyway, I fell in love."

"With one of the bikinis?"

"With Malibu. There's something about it." He slowly shook his head. "I can't describe it to you. If you feel it, you'll know what I mean. It took awhile, but I finally found a place right on the beach. Cost me a fortune, but it's worth every penny to see the sunrise over the ocean."

While he described the area to her, Paige realized he hadn't dropped a single name. He must have famous neighbors, but he didn't mention them. For Nick, the allure of Malibu had nothing to do with prestige or celebrity. The ocean itself had drawn him there.

She loved him more all the time.

* * *

Paige stood in the middle of his living room staring out the wall of towering glass doors at the ocean.

"Oh, Nick. It's beautiful."

She walked right past the expensive rugs and furniture the decorator had assured him would turn any head with a female brain in it. Nick followed her onto the deck and down the steps to the beach. She stood on the wind-sculpted sand, watching the last rays of the sun drop below the horizon.

A flock of gulls passed overhead, and Paige tipped her head back to smile up at them. He watched in amazement as she closed her eyes, held out her arms, and took a deep breath.

The sight of her embracing the place he loved was almost more than he could take.

Trying to sound casual, he asked, "Like it?"

"It's wonderful. I can see why you love it here."

"I knew you would. The first time I came out here, I knew I was home. Bought the house without even asking the price."

When she laughed, he joined her. "Yeah, not exactly a shrewd business move, but I've never regretted it." He looked back at the gray-washed clapboard house. "It's great, but it needs something. Maybe while you're here, you can figure it out."

"You mean, because I'm a woman?"

"No." Draping an arm around her shoulders, he walked her back up the steps. "Because you're smart, and you don't live here. I like your place. It's cozy and inviting."

"And small."

"Gimme a break. How much space do you need? You only take up a couple of square feet at a time."

"I like this." She spread her arms as she slowly spun in the middle of the vaulted great room. "You could put a twenty-foot Christmas tree in here."

"Maybe that's what it needs."

Paige nailed him with one of her looks. The kind that meant trouble. "You don't put up a tree, do you?"

"Mom does two. Does that count?"

"I bet you don't even hang a wreath on the door or put up mistletoe."

"Guilty," he chuckled, heading for the fridge. "Can I get you anything?"

"No, thanks." She took a picture from the rough-hewn redwood mantel. "These are your parents?"

He nodded, sipping his water as she set the frame back in place. She worked her way around the room, pausing here and there to ask him questions. Fascinated, he settled on the wide plank steps to watch her. When she got to the closed doors leading to his study, she paused and looked over her shoulder at him.

"Can I go in?"

"If you want. I'll warn you, it's a mess."

"Is that why the doors are closed?"

Nick crossed the room to open them for her. "Why else?"

Her ingenuous blue eyes studied him for a long moment. "I thought maybe you didn't want me in there."

A few months ago, he wouldn't have, but during the time they'd spent together, she'd opened up a lot more than the doors to his study. "Well, you share your house with me, and I really like it. Now it's my turn."

She smiled, and Nick felt another piece of his heart desert him. Shrugging off his sudden fit of uncertainty, he snapped on the lights and waited for her reaction.

His worktable was stacked with reference books and pads full of notes that sometimes even he couldn't read. The built-in bookcases were crammed with novels and books with titles like *Murder, Mayhem and Madness*. Dozens of newspapers were stacked in bins. He used the articles to help make his fictional crimes realistic.

"I like it in here. This is you. Creative, full of words and ideas." Then she frowned. "Where are your awards?"

"Anita's office. She likes to show off, so I let her take them. Nobody sees 'em here."

"How many do you have?"

"A few."

Paige gave him a knowing smile. "You don't know, do you?"

"Got me there," he chuckled. "There's something in here for you, by the way."

"Really?" She glanced around again, looking perplexed. "Where?"

"On the desk."

Humming quietly, a laptop computer displayed the rolling message *Time After Time*.

She gasped. "No way. I thought that was yours."

"You said if you had a computer, you could write more stories for Hannah," he reminded her. "I read the ones you sent me, and I think other kids would enjoy them, too. If you want, I'll show them to Anita."

"I hardly think I need an agent."

One minute she was laughing, and the next she looked deadly serious, her eyes fixed on the storyboard mounted beside his desk. She stared at the divorce decree for a few seconds, then glared at him. "Is there a point to this?"

"Just a reminder."

"Of what?"

Her voice had taken on a sharp edge, and he chose his words carefully. "Mistakes I've made. I don't want to make them again."

The proud sparkle had left his eyes, and he'd pulled away from her. Not much, but she felt it all the same, and she doubted he was aware of it. "What kind of mistakes?"

"Do we really have to fight about this now?"

"Yes, we do. You can't keep punishing yourself for things in the past. You're missing so much by looking at where you've been instead of where you could go."

"What? You didn't see this?" He snatched the *New York Times* from the desk and waved it at her. "Number five this week."

She took the paper from him and set it on his cluttered worktable. "That's not you. That's what you do. You're an awesome writer, and people love your books."

"*You* love my books."

His tone sounded accusing, but in his eyes she saw that wounded little boy, begging her to tell him he was wrong.

"No, Nick," she murmured, resting her hand on his jaw. "I enjoy your books, but I love you."

Gratitude flashed in his eyes before he masked it with a chuckle. "Keep talking like that, I won't let you leave."

She knew he was testing her, and she took it as graciously as she could. Nick's perspective made him wary of everyone, downright mistrustful of women. Slipping her arms around his waist, she smiled up at him. "Maybe I don't want to."

When his eyes met hers, they were a soft blue. His voice was even softer. "I love the way you look at me."

"How is that?"

"Like you honestly want to be here with me."

"There's no place else I'd rather be."

She felt the warmth of his skin through his shirt. As the tenderness in his eyes began to simmer, her heart skipped several beats. Cupping her chin, he traced her lips with his thumb, then leaned in for a kiss that ended way too soon.

"Come on." He stepped back to take her hand. "I'll show you upstairs so you can get settled."

* * *

Nick was passing the guest room when he heard Paige's laughter.

"What?"

She turned and held up a leopard-print chemise. Pinned to it was a note that read *GRRR*.

"Brenda," she said. With a flirtatious smile, she dangled it in front of her. "What do you think? Is it me?"

"Why don't you try it on and see?"

After a surprised look, she scampered into the bathroom. He shoved his hands in his pockets and stared out the balcony doors, waiting for his better judgment to assert itself.

It never did.

The bathroom door opened, and Paige held her arms wide. "Well?"

Fighting a smile, Nick motioned for her to spin around so he could see the back. What there was of it, anyway. "It's unique, I'll say that much. You missed this."

He slid a finger under the strap to straighten it, following it from her shoulder down to the plunging waistline. As his knuckle brushed the small of her back, he felt her shiver.

She turned to face him, flashing him a playful smile. "Do you like it?"

"I would've bought you something different."

Dangling her arms over his shoulders, she pressed into him. Soft, inviting curves melted against him, backed up by a sultry smile.

"Which do you prefer? Satin or silk?"

"I like silk." As he traced the low scoop neckline, her pulse raced under his touch, nudging him another step closer to the edge.

"Lace?"

"I like lace," he murmured, leaning in to taste the delicious smile curving her lips. When he realized she was easing him toward the four-poster bed, he drew away. But not very far.

"Paige, are you sure?"

"I'm sure."

He kissed her, for the first time bringing her closer instead of holding her at a safe distance. Soft tendrils of warmth radiated through him and finally, he surrendered.

"I love you, Paige."

She kept a straight face for about three seconds, and he laughed. "You already knew, didn't you?"

"Yeah."

"Hope you don't get tired of hearing it."

"Never."

In her eyes shimmered all the things he'd been missing, and she stole the last piece of his heart with a kiss.

Chapter Nine

"**P**retty night," Paige commented, leaning on the balcony railing.

He nosed her hair aside to kiss her bare shoulder. "Mmm-hmm."

She turned to face him. "Nick, this was such a nice Christmas present, coming to Jamaica again. Thank you."

"You're welcome." From the table, he took a box wrapped in gold foil topped with a frothy white bow. "This is for you, too."

His voice rippled with barely contained excitement, and Paige gasped. "Your book!"

"Just open it."

The cover showed an elegant parchment with pictures of old-fashioned clocks and pocket watches. Superimposed over them were drawings of the Golden Gate Bridge and Big Ben. *Time After Time* cut diagonally across the front in gilded script and, in the lower right corner, Nick's sprawling signature was embossed in more gold.

The cover alone must have cost a fortune, but it sure would stand out in the bookstores. Paige imagined opening cartons of these books, placing them on the shelves while her heart burst with pride for what he'd accomplished.

"Nick, it's beautiful. Really, really classy."

"It's an advance copy. I wanted you to have one, to thank you for all your help."

"Oh, you're welcome. It was awesome to be the first person to read it."

She flipped the book over, admiring the sepia-toned picture of him staring out at the ocean. Then she read the splashy jacket summary and his little bio. There was a time when that was all she knew about him. It was only months ago, but it seemed a lot longer. When she turned to the dedication page, her heart skipped several beats.

There, in simple brown type, were two words.

For Paige.

She stared at them in disbelief, then up at him. "You dedicated your book to me?"

"Never would've written it if I hadn't met you."

"But you were working on it when you met me."

"On part of it, sure. But all that stuff with Derek and Ellen." He took her cheek in his hand and slowly shook his head, as if he still didn't quite believe it. "I couldn't write that before you. I didn't have it in me."

"Yes, you did. You just didn't know it."

Nick gently kissed her. "Sweet Paige. You believed in me even when I didn't believe in myself. You made me want to dream and make wishes on stars." Taking her left hand, Nick slipped on the dainty ring he'd had designed for her. Her delighted smile drove his carefully rehearsed proposal right out of his head. So he improvised.

"Marry me, Paige. Come share my ocean with me."

She flung her arms around him, simultaneously laughing and crying as only women seemed to do.

"Is that a yes?" When she nodded, he smiled. "May I ask you something?"

Wiping her cheeks, her voice shaking with excitement, she said, "You just asked me to marry you. What else is there?"

"Last time we were here, the night we went walking on the beach. What did you wish for?"

Love and laughter shone in her eyes as she kissed him.

"I wished for you."

~END~

About the Author

Andrea Wilder lives in Upstate New York with her husband and two children. With an abiding interest in just about everything, she reads widely but especially enjoys romance because she likes happy endings.

Andrea writes contemporary and historical fiction with an occasional diversion into fantasy. A member of Romance Writers of America, she holds Bachelors of Arts degrees in English Writing and Political Science. When she's not writing, she works part-time as a bookkeeper and office assistant for a consulting firm.

If you'd like to know more, you can stop by *www.andreawilder.com.* While you're there, send Andrea an email. She'd love to hear from you.